For Clever Eric,
cake lover and storyteller
extraordinaire—C.F.

For Anne and Lee—G.B.K.

Text copyright © 2010 by Candace Fleming
Illustrations copyright © 2010 by G. Brian Karas
All rights reserved. Published in the United States
by Schwartz & Wade Books, an imprint of
Random House Children's Books,
a division of Random House, Inc., New York.
Schwartz & Wade Books and the colophon
are trademarks of Random House, Inc.
Visit us on the Web! www.randomhouse.com/kids
Educators and librarians, for a variety of teaching tools,
visit us at www.randomhouse.com/teachers
Library of Congress Cataloging-in-Publication Data
Fleming, Candace.
Clever Jack takes the cake / Candace Fleming ;
illustrated by G. Brian Karas.—1st ed.   p. cm.

Summary: A poor boy named Jack
struggles to deliver a birthday present
worthy of the princess.
ISBN 978-0-375-84979-4 (trade) —
ISBN 978-0-375-95697-3 (lib. bdg.)
[1. Fairy tales.] I. Karas, G. Brian, ill. II. Title.
PZ8.F5775Cl 2010
[E]—dc22
2009030030
The text of this book is set in Archetype.
The illustrations are rendered
in gouache and pencil.
MANUFACTURED IN CHINA
10 9 8 7 6 5 4 3 2 1
First Edition

CLEVER JACK
TAKES the CAKE

WRITTEN by CANDACE FLEMING

ILLUSTRATED by G. BRIAN KARAS

schwartz & wade books · new york

One summer morning long ago, a poor boy named Jack found an invitation slipped beneath his cottage door. It read:

His Majesty the King

cordially invites
all the children of the Realm
to
the Princess's Tenth Birthday
Party
tomorrow afternoon
in the Castle Courtyard

"A party!" exclaimed Jack. "For the princess!"
His mother sighed. "What a shame you can't go."
"Why not?" asked Jack.
"Because we've nothing fine enough to give her,"
his mother replied. "And no money to buy a gift."

Jack had to admit his mother was right. His pockets were empty except for the matchsticks he always carried. As for their few belongings—a spinning wheel, a threadbare quilt, a pitted ax— what princess wanted those?

The boy thought a moment. "Then I will make her something," he declared. "I will make her a cake."

"From what?" asked his mother. "From the dust in the cupboard? From the dirt on the floor?"

"I have a better idea," said Jack.

And that same morning,
he traded his ax for two
bags of sugar, and his
quilt for a sack of flour.

He gave the hen an extra handful of
seed in exchange for two fresh eggs,

and he kissed the cow on
the nose for a pail of her
sweetest milk.

He gathered walnuts.

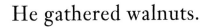

He dipped candles.

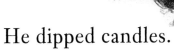

And in the strawberry patch, he searched . . . and searched . . . and searched until he found the reddest, juiciest, most succulent strawberry in the land.

"Delicious!"

said Jack as he plucked it from its stem.

Then he set to work, churning, chopping, blending, baking.

That same night, Jack stood back to admire his creation—two layers of golden-sweet cake covered in buttery frosting and ringed with ten tiny candles. Across the cake's top, walnuts spelled out "Happy Birthday, Princess." And in the very center—in the place of honor—sat the succulent strawberry.

"What a fine, fine gift," said Jack's mother. Jack grinned.

Early the next morning, with combed hair and clean shirt, Jack set off for the castle, holding the cake proudly before him.

Before long, he came to a bloom-speckled meadow.

Perhaps I should pick a bouquet for the princess, thought Jack, just as four-and-twenty blackbirds rose into the air. Like a sudden summer storm cloud, they swirled around the cake, pecking, nipping, flapping, picking.

"Get back!" hollered Jack.

"I'm taking this cake to the princess."

"Aw-caw-caw-caw-caw!" cackled the birds.

And as quickly as they had come, they were gone, taking with
them the walnuts that spelled "Happy Birthday, Princess."

Jack looked at his gift. "At least I still have two layers of cake, ten candles, and the succulent strawberry," he said. Holding the cake proudly before him, Jack continued on to the castle.

Before long, he came to a bridge.

"Toll!" a voice demanded.

Out stepped a wild-haired troll. "No one crosses my bridge without paying."

"But I haven't any money," said Jack.

The troll licked his lips. "But you do have a cake."

"I'm taking this to the princess," said Jack.

"And just how will you get it there?" growled the troll. "You and your cake are on *this* side of the river. The princess is on *that* side, and my bridge is the *only* way across."

Jack considered the problem. "I will make you a deal. If you let me cross, I will give you half this cake."

"Agreed," grunted the troll.

So Jack slid out one layer and, as the troll slobbered and gobbled, crossed the bridge.

On the other side, he looked down at his gift. "At least I still have a layer of cake, ten candles, and the succulent strawberry," he said.

Holding the cake proudly before him, Jack continued on to the castle.

Before long he came to the forest. No birds chirped here. No squirrels chittered.

As if under a spell, the entire wood lay silent, sleeping. Only the wind seemed to whisper, "Beware! Beware!"

Pulling the cake closer, Jack pressed on.

The road grew narrower. The trees grew thicker. The light grew dimmer. Soon it was so dark that Jack couldn't see the cake in front of his face.

"Turn back!" the wind whispered. "Turn back!"

"I can't!" cried Jack. "I'm taking this cake to the princess."

And he reached into his pocket for a matchstick, struck
it on his shoe, and lit one of the ten candles.

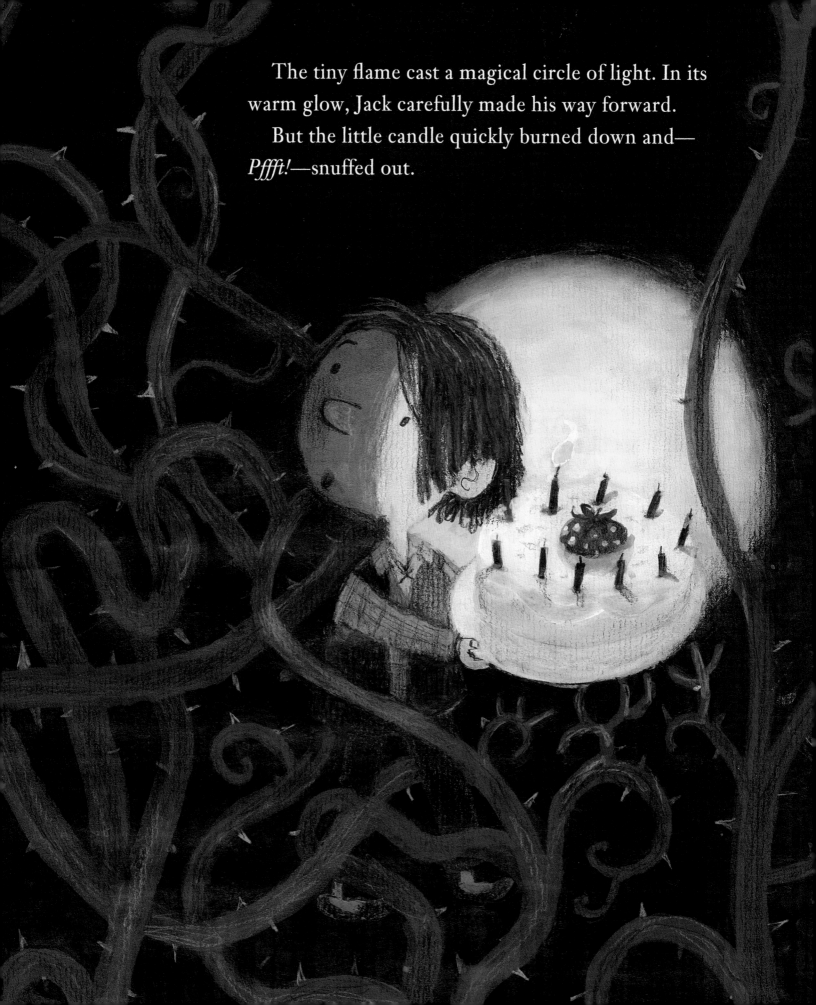

The tiny flame cast a magical circle of light. In its
warm glow, Jack carefully made his way forward.
But the little candle quickly burned down and—
Pffft!—snuffed out.

So Jack lit a second candle.

But he had not gone much farther before—
Pffft!—it, too, snuffed out.

So Jack lit a third . . . then a fourth . . . then a
fifth . . . until the tenth and final candle flickered,
fluttered, sputtered to its end.

And as it did, the road widened, the trees thinned, and
the bright sunlight shone once more.

Jack looked down at his gift. "At least I still have a layer
of cake and the succulent strawberry," he said.

Holding the cake proudly before him, Jack continued on to the castle.

Before long he came to a clearing.

"Good morning, young sir!" called out an old gypsy woman. "Have you come to see Samson dance?"

At the sound of his name, the bear beside her rose up on his hind legs.

"I don't have time," replied Jack. "I'm taking this cake to the princess."

"Then we shall make it a quick jig," said the gypsy, snatching up her concertina.

Oompa-oompa! wheezed the instrument.

Shuffle-shuffle-kick, danced the bear.

Tap-tap-tap, went Jack's foot, as he set down the cake to dance with his new friends.

G-U-U-U-L-P!

"Hey," cried Jack, "that bear ate the princess's cake!"

"PAT

OOIE!"

"But not the strawberry," said the gypsy.
"Samson hates fruit."

Jack looked down at his gift, and for several seconds he was unable to speak. Finally, he said, "At least I still have this—the reddest, juiciest, most succulent strawberry in the land."

And holding the strawberry proudly before him, Jack continued on to the castle.
Across the drawbridge . . .
Through the fortress walls . . .

. . . Straight into the courtyard.

What a sight! There, smack in the center of all the merry festivities, sat the princess on her velvet throne, a long line of guests stretched before her. One by one, they presented her with their gifts, each more fabulous than the last.

But even the most magnificent treasures did not seem to interest Her Highness. "More rubies?" she said with a bored yawn. "How tiresome. Another tiara? How dull."

Joining the line, Jack glanced down at his humble gift.

"And just what have you brought the princess?" a guard asked from behind him.

"A strawberry," said Jack. "The reddest, juiciest, most succulent one in the land." He held it out for the guard to see.

"That is a fine piece of fruit," agreed the guard. "But I cannot allow you to give it to the princess."

"Why not?" asked Jack.

"Because she is allergic to strawberries," said the guard. "One taste and she swells up like a balloon."

"No!" gasped Jack.

"Yes," said the guard. "I'm sorry, but you'll have to give it to me."
Reluctantly, Jack handed over the strawberry.

"*Mmmmm.*"

Now Jack found himself at the front of the line.

The princess turned her gaze to him. "And what have *you* brought me?" she asked.

Jack gulped. He blushed. He shuffled his feet.

"Well?"

Jack took a deep breath and knelt down before her.

"Your Highness," he began, "let me explain what happened."

And he told the princess about trading for
the ingredients to bake a golden-sweet cake
just for her. He told her about the swirling
storm of blackbirds, the wild-haired troll, and
the dark, dark wood. He told her about the old
gypsy woman and her concertina, and the bear
who loved to dance but hated fruit.

"And in the end," said Jack, "I still had the
succulent strawberry, but . . ." The boy sighed.
"You're allergic to strawberries."

He waited for her to yawn.

"So the guard ate it," he concluded.

The princess laughed and clapped her hands in delight.

"A story!"

she exclaimed. "And an adventure story at that! What a fine gift."

Then the princess rose from her throne and proclaimed, "Time for birthday cake. And my new friend Jack shall have the honor of cutting it."

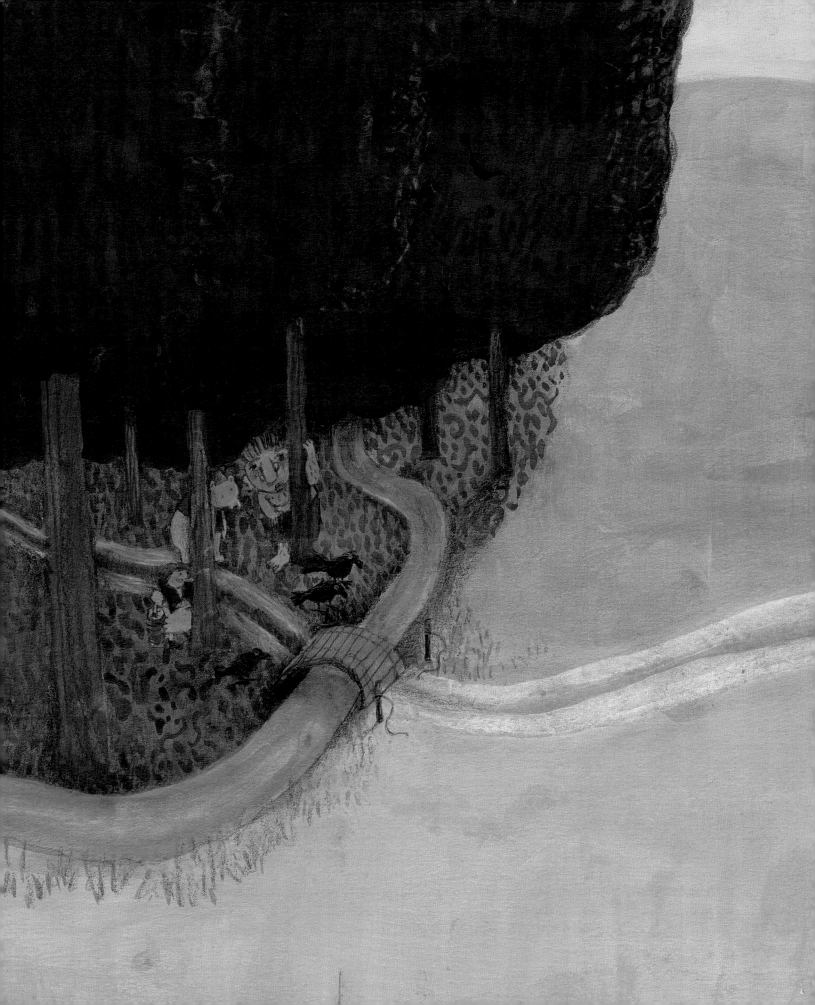